For K & E, and for the Folly Farm Gang
– A.L.

For Mum
– L.B.

The Magic Potions Shop

The Young Apprentice

www.randomhousechildrens.co.uk

Chapter One

In the Kingdom of Arthwen,
  there was a very unusual shop.
It wasn't on the high street;
  it was deep in the forest.
It wasn't in a building;
  it was inside a tree.
It didn't sell food, or clothes,
  or toys: this shop sold potions.

People travelled from miles around
to find the old tree in Steadysong

Forest. It was
the biggest tree
in the land and its
enormous branches
stretched up to the sky.
At the base of the tree,
inside the hollowed-
out trunk, was the
Potions Shop, its wooden
shelves creaking from the
weight of thousands of jars
and bottles and pots. Fairies came
there to get **Glitter Dust** to make
them shine. Princes popped in for
Handsome Cream to make them
look their very best. And Cloud
Giants bought **Growth** Potion
to put into their babies' bottles.

Above
the shop,
at the top of
the tree, was
where Tibben and
Grandpa lived.

Grandpa was the Potions Master.
He was ninety-nine years old and
Tibben thought he was wonderful.
He might look small and wrinkly
and frail, but Grandpa was so
powerful! He could mix something
to make you speak cat, something
to make you six metres tall, or

something to make Brussels sprouts taste like ice cream.

Grandpa travelled up and down the kingdom, helping creatures from the Frozen Tundra in the north to the Parched Desert in the south. He had been the Potions Master for many years and his cloak sparkled with Glints, the magical signs of potions skills. Each Glint was different in size and shape and colour: some shone with a blue-green pearly light; some were tiny bright dots; others glowed the deep orange or brown of the rocks.

Tibben wanted to be a Potions Master just like Grandpa one day, but for now he was an Apprentice.

He spent all day
climbing up and down
the rickety old ladders
in the shop, fetching

liquids,

gases,

powders,

pastes,

creams,

ointments,

seeds,

bones,

leaves,

and
flower fluff

to help Grandpa mix his magic.
In return, Grandpa taught Tibben
all about potions.

Grandpa knew that one day Tibben would be a wonderful Potions Master. But Tibben wasn't so sure. His training wasn't going very well. Not one of his potions had worked, and he hadn't earned a single **Glint** for his plain green cloak.

His **Camouflage Potion** had left his hands covered in bright purple spots.

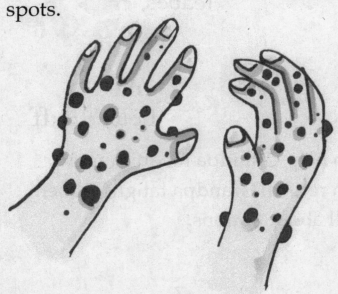

His *Invisible* **Potion** had made him glow in the dark. And his **Growth** **Potion** had only worked on his nose! Three birds had built a little nest there, right at the end, and had stayed a whole week.

Tibben sighed. When would he get his first **Glint**?

"Stop worrying about **Glints** all the time," Grandpa told him. "Potion-making is about *helping*. You'll get your first **Glint** one day."

"When I finally make a potion that works," said Tibben grumpily.

"No, when you make a potion that *helps*," said Grandpa. "Then the **Glint** will appear, right

there on your cloak." He pointed.
"In the meantime you just need
practice; practice and confidence."

Tibben rubbed his cloak between
his fingers. It was hard to believe
he would ever be a Potions Master.

Chapter Two

The next morning Tibben woke
in his little bed, in his little round
room at the very top of the tree. He
climbed down the spiral stairs to
the shop below, where Grandpa was
waiting with a cup of Hazelwood
tea and a potions recipe to practise.

Tibben had been working on
Flying Potion all week.

"Right" – Grandpa slurped his
tea – "have another go."

"OK," said Tibben nervously.
He reached under
the wooden counter
and pulled out a
heavy book with a
red leather cover.
On the front, in
bumpy gold
writing, were
the words: *The
Book of Potions*.

"Now remember, Tibben," said
Grandpa, "mixing potions isn't
just about following the recipe. It's
about—"

"I know, Grandpa," Tibben
interrupted. "'The recipe is just
a guide'." He had heard his

Grandpa's explanation a hundred times.

"That's right," said Grandpa patiently. "Listen to the potion. Give it what it needs and feel your way."

Tibben nodded, but in truth he had no idea what Grandpa meant. How do you listen to a potion? Tibben wished Grandpa would just tell him exactly what to do. After all, the last time Tibben had made Flying Potion, he had added too much Cloud Lotus and had made Rain Potion by mistake. The shop had been flooded all morning and the Oil Ants had been forced to swim to the counter to place their orders for Trail Powder.

"Every potion works differently for every Potions Master," Grandpa continued. "You have to balance the mixture. Maybe the very thing the potion needs is not in the recipe."

Tibben shook his head in bewilderment, but Grandpa just smiled.

"Why don't you go and get the ingredients while I finish my tea?"

Tibben turned to page 53 of *The Book of Potions*. It read:

FLYING POTION

EFFECT: Allows flight of up to 30 metres for a period of 15 minutes.
INGREDIENTS: Light Puff, Cloud Lotus, Golden Root.

He went to collect what he needed.

Cloud Lotus was a fluffy plant that grew in the middle of Lake Sapphire. In the shop it was stored in a fish tank just above the counter.

Light Puff was very rare. It came from the breath of a dragon. In the Potions Shop it was kept on the ceiling. Up, up, up Tibben climbed until he was on the top rung of the wooden ladder. He stretched out a small silver net and scooped up some floating wisps.

Golden Root grew underground in Moonlight Meadow. Grandpa had picked some last time he went there to help the fairies. Now it

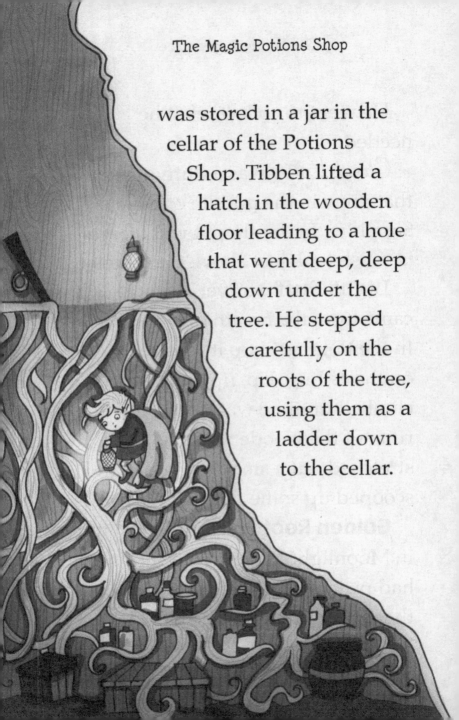

was stored in a jar in the
cellar of the Potions
Shop. Tibben lifted a
hatch in the wooden
floor leading to a hole
that went deep, deep
down under the
tree. He stepped
carefully on the
roots of the tree,
using them as a
ladder down
to the cellar.

By the time he got back, Grandpa had fallen asleep.

Tibben touched his arm. "Grandpa. I'm ready to start."

"Oh, good." Grandpa yawned.

Tibben put his training bowl on the counter. It was made of an enormous **Mage Nut** from a tree in Steadysong Forest. Grandpa had taken him to choose the nut years ago, when he was only a little pixie, and together they had cut it in half to make the special bowl.

Now Tibben added all the ingredients. He ground the **Golden Root** and added some wisps of **Light Puff**. Then he squeezed the *Cloud Lotus* until all its liquid came out. He mixed and mixed until he had a cup of bright golden potion.

"What do you think, Grandpa?"

Grandpa looked at him kindly. "What do *you* think?"

"Um . . . I don't know."

"Well," said Grandpa, "let's see if it works."

Nervously Tibben raised the potion to his lips. The drink tingled on his tongue. His tummy felt all warm inside as the liquid started to fizz.

"Yes!" he shouted. "It's working! I can feel it!"

Grandpa smiled.

"I'm going to fly! I'm sure of it!" cried Tibben. But—

"Whoa!" Something strange was happening.

"What is it?" said Grandpa.

"Look!" Tibben's feet had turned bright yellow. He watched as his toes began to grow, stretching like roots into the cracks between the floorboards.

"I'm stuck!" cried Tibben. "What's happening?"

"I think," said Grandpa calmly, "instead of making **Flying Potion**, you've made *Rooting Potion*."

"*Rooting Potion*? What's that?"

"It sticks your feet to the floor," said Grandpa. "It's the opposite of **Flying Potion**."

Tibben wobbled this way and that. "How could I have got it so wrong?"

"You must have stirred the mixture backwards."

"Why didn't you tell me, Grandpa?" said Tibben crossly.

"Because it's better to learn these things for yourself." Grandpa ruffled Tibben's hair. "Don't worry. It took

me years to make **Flying Potion**.
Years! You just have to keep trying."

Tibben sighed. Now he'd have
to stand there for two hours and
fifteen minutes until the *Rooting
Potion* had finally worn off.

That night Tibben sat on the bed,
staring at *The Book of Potions*.
He really wanted to be able to help
everyone and
everything, just
like Grandpa
did. *Please –*
he crossed his
fingers – *please
let me earn
a* **Glint**.

From the window came the
honking of a flock of Star Geese.
Tibben looked up to see them flying
in and out of the trees. The sun was
setting on the distant Lake Sapphire
and its sleepy light filtered through
the forest. Tibben watched as the

geese turned on the breeze, heading north towards the Frozen Tundra. Looking at the view before him, Tibben slowly began to feel happy and warm.

"Tomorrow I'll try again," he told himself.

Chapter Three

When he woke in the morning, Tibben knew that something was wrong. The tree was very quiet. Normally he could hear the clink of jars or the scrape of china as Grandpa set out ingredients and ground seeds into powders. But not this morning.

Tibben made a cup of Hazelwood tea and took it up for Grandpa. He knocked on the door of Grandpa's bedroom.

"Grandpa?"

"Come in," he croaked.

Tibben opened the door to find him lying in bed. "Are you OK, Grandpa?"

"I'm just tired," he sighed. "I'm ninety-nine now. Nearly a hundred. It's almost time for me to finish

being the Potions Master." Grandpa
ruffled Tibben's hair again. "You
know that, don't you, Tibben?"

"Yes, Grandpa," said Tibben, but
in truth he had tried not to think
about it. "Does that mean you will
go away for ever?"

"No." Grandpa smiled. "I'm
going to retire to a lovely cottage in
the Vale of Years. It's in the east, just
past the Troll Hills. You can come
and visit me there." He looked at
Tibben closely. "But it does mean
that it will be time for a new Potions
Master to take over."

"A new Potions Master?" said
Tibben. "So will someone else train
me?"

"No, Tibben," said Grandpa softly. "I mean *you*. You need to be the next Potions Master."

"Me?" Tibben shifted nervously from one foot to another. "But I'm just the Apprentice."

"Well, we have time. Not a lot of time, it's true. But enough time for you to learn—"

"Learn to be a Potions Master?" interrupted Tibben.

"Yes."

"Before you turn a hundred?"

"Yes."

Tibben looked down. He fingered

the fabric of his cloak. There was something he had to know.

"What if . . . ?" he said in a small voice. "What if I can't do it in time?"

"You'll do it," said Grandpa. "I know you will."

"But what if I don't?"

Grandpa closed his eyes.

"Please, Grandpa, please tell me! What if, when you turn a hundred, I'm not ready to be the Potions Master?"

Grandpa didn't speak for a little while. Then, when he did, his voice was soft and low.

"In Arthwen there are two energies at work," he said. "One is Harmony. Harmony is the natural world as it should be: rivers flowing, seasons changing and flowers blossoming. You know, Tibben, how you sometimes look at the sun rising over Steadysong Forest, or the stars twinkling in the blue-black sky, and you feel happy and warm?" Tibben nodded. "Well, that's Harmony."

"What's the other energy, Grandpa?" Tibben was listening closely.

"The other energy is called Blight," said Grandpa. "Blight is destruction. It is what makes the plants die and the rivers dry up. It is a strange feeling of sadness and fear and

emptiness; when you think nothing can go right and everything seems wrong."

Tibben shivered. "I don't like the sound of Blight," he said.

"No," said Grandpa, "but Blight is what makes our work so important. The help we give is what holds back Blight. Every time we help someone, every time we make something better, Harmony grows."

"And you get a Glint," said Tibben.

"Yes," said Grandpa, "but that's not so important. What is *most* important is that Blight is stopped and Harmony grows."

Tibben's eyes grew wide. He suddenly realized what Grandpa meant.

"So if there's no Potions Master . . ." he began.

"Blight will grow," said Grandpa firmly. "The air will fill with mist and sadness. The plants will wither and the animals will go hungry."

Tibben stood up. "But how do I do it?" he said, "How do I become a Potions Master?"

"You keep practising. You keep learning," said Grandpa. "One day you'll get your first Glint. Then another and another. And when you have five, you'll take the Master's

Challenge. If you pass, then you'll be a Potions Master too."

Tibben stared at Grandpa. *Five* **Glints**! *Five* **Glints** *and then a big test?*

Grandpa took his hand. "You can do it, Tibben," he said, swinging his legs out of bed. "I'll come downstairs and help you. You can practise all day."

Tibben nodded, but inside he was worried.

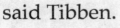

The bluebell of the Potions Shop rang out.

"Our first customer of the day," cried Grandpa, pulling on his cloak. "Down you go! Here's your chance to help."

At the counter was Snark, a Thunder Goblin from the Diamond Mines.

"Good morning," said Tibben.

"Mornin'," said Snark in his rough voice. "We're having some trouble in the mines today. There's been a rock fall in Blue Mountain and we can't get through."

"Um . . ." said Tibben. He opened *The Book of Potions* and thumbed through the pages. He could sense Grandpa watching him from the bottom of the stairs.

Under E Tibben found:

Exploding Powder

INGREDIENTS:
Jumping Flint
Fire Seeds
Red-Hot Orchid

"Good," said Grandpa. "I'll get the ingredients and you make the potion." He opened the box of

Jumping Flint. "Whoops!" he cried as pebbles of flint leaped into the air. Grandpa managed to catch one and handed it to Tibben, who held it down with a heavy hammer.

"Don't mind me! You carry on!" cried Grandpa as he hopped around the shop trying to catch the rest of the escaped pebbles.

Tibben concentrated hard on the recipe. With special gloves he put the *Fire Seeds* into his **Mage Nut** bowl.

"How much **Red-Hot Orchid,** Grandpa?"

"Can't hear you," puffed Grandpa, chasing a piece of flint.

"Um . . ." Tibben turned the

Red-Hot Orchid over in his hands. He peeled off some of the ruby-coloured petals and added them to the seeds. Then he held the *Jumping Flint* with one hand and lifted the hammer:

Smash!

He grabbed the tiny pieces of pebble leaping about and shoved them into the bowl as fast as he could, mixing them until they became a rippling powder.

"I think I've finished," said Tibben, looking at the deep red dust.

"OK," said Grandpa. He came back to the table. "Test it on this twig," he said. "Just try a tiny bit."

Snark the goblin
stood back while Tibben
tipped the bowl and
dripped a teeny drop
onto the twig. All at once
the twig stood up on its
end and began to dance
about, spinning and
hopping in the air.

"Ah," said Grandpa.
"A bit too much
Jumping Flint. You've made a
Fire Dance Potion there."

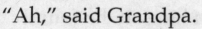

Snark snarled.

"Try again," said Grandpa.

"No way!" said Tibben, glancing
at the angry Thunder Goblin. "You
make it, Grandpa."

Grandpa sighed. "You help
the next customer, then," he said.
"Don't forget to test potions before
you send them out. Have a little sip
yourself if you can."

But Tibben didn't manage to help
anyone all day.

He tried to make *Super Speeding
Potion* for a Racing Snail, but when
he tested it on himself, he found
he had somehow made **Ten Legs
Potion**.

"Try again," said Grandpa.

"Never!" said Tibben. "I kept
kicking myself in the bum."

When a Silver Squirrel came in
wanting **High Reach Potion** for
picking nuts at the top of trees,

Tibben accidentally made **Arm Stretch Cream,** meant for giant squid.

"Have another go," said Grandpa, trying not to laugh at Tibben's hugely long arms.

"No," said Tibben, trying to fold his arms away. "I won't get it right. You make it, Grandpa."

Grandpa sighed and reached for his bowl again.

Chapter Four

A few days later Tibben was at the
top of the highest ladder, putting
away the Shrinking Potion, when a
large dog bounded into the shop.
It was Padge – one of King Krono's
messengers. Padge barked and
showed Tibben the note
attached to his
collar.

Dear Potions Master,

We need your help!

There is a horrible howling in Western Valley. It is the growl of a terrible monster. The brave knights are too scared to fight it. The witches fainted when they heard it. And the soldiers all cried for their mummies. Please help us!

There is a strange mist in the air. The rocks are sliding away. The plants are withering. And the animals are restless.

Your potions are our only hope.

Tibben rushed straight upstairs.
"Grandpa, Grandpa!" Tibben
showed him the letter. "What's
happening? Is it Blight? Do you
think it's Blight?" He was starting to
panic.

Grandpa stood up from his
reading chair and reached into a
secret pocket of his cloak. He drew
out a strange object that Tibben had
never seen before. It looked like an

old pocket watch. Grandpa flicked it open and the device made a humming noise.

"What's that?" asked Tibben.

"This is the *Master's Dial*," said Grandpa. "It measures Harmony and Blight." At the top of the dial, at twelve o'clock, was a large golden H. At the bottom, at six o'clock, was a B. Grandpa showed Tibben a thin brown arrow. It was pointing just past Harmony, in the ten-past position.

"Hmm," said Grandpa. "There are signs of Blight."

Tibben gave a shiver. "What are you going to do, Grandpa?"

"You mean, what are *you* going to do?" said Grandpa.

"Me?"

"Oh, Tibben, Western Valley is a long way and I'm too tired and old to go that far," said Grandpa. He leaned back and closed his eyes.

"But I haven't even got my first Glint!" cried Tibben. His heart was pounding. "Grandpa, I'm not ready! I haven't practised enough. I don't know enough about potions. I don't know enough about Harmony. I can't help!"

Grandpa opened his eyes. "You *can* help," he said calmly.

"I know you can. And helping creatures is what will bring back Harmony."

"But . . ."

"Now off you go." Grandpa settled back on his pillow. "Don't forget to look for potion ingredients, especially new ones. A good Potions Master will always find a way to make use of them." He took a breath. "And remember, Tibben, the most powerful ingredients are those that are given in kindness or gratitude."

Tibben rushed downstairs. As quickly as he could, he packed a bag full of Grandpa's already-mixed

potions. *At least these ones will work*, he thought to himself. He grabbed his **Mage Nut** bowl and *The Book of Potions*.

"I hope I can do this," he said to himself. "I hope I can help."

Tibben looked around the Potions Shop one last time. His fingers scrunched the edge of his

plain green cloak and he made a
wish under his breath. Then he
closed the door and set off.

Up at the top of the tree, Grandpa
watched Tibben till he disappeared
deep into the forest.

"Good luck," he whispered.

Chapter Five

The journey to Western Valley
was long. First Tibben walked
westwards through Steadysong
Forest. Then he waded through
Bubble River and over the bank
till he came to the beautiful Lake
Sapphire. He had often been here
with Grandpa, to collect **Red Clay**
for **Sticking Potion**, and he loved
watching the Silver Fish dancing
under the clear blue water.

By the side of the lake Tibben saw
Marina Mermaid sitting on a rock
combing her long green hair.

"Oh, Potions Apprentice!" she
called. "Thank goodness you are
here. I can't swim fast enough to join
my friends. Do you have something
to make my tail stronger?"

"Hmm." Tibben
gave her a jar
of Grandpa's
Growth Potion.

"Thank you," said
Marina, and she
swam to the centre of
the lake to pick him a *Cloud Lotus* in
return.

"Thank you," said Tibben.

In the Cave of Darkness Tibben
met Darnöf the dragon.

"Ah, Potions Apprentice," he said.

"Thank goodness you are here. My belly flame has stopped working." Tibben thought for a moment

and gave him one of
Grandpa's **Magic Coals.**

"Thank you," said Darnöf.
"Please fill your jar with my
Light Puff."

"Thank you," said Tibben.

In Moonlight Meadow a Specs Mole
called Wisgar had a broken claw.

Tibben pulled out Grandpa's **Tidy
Thread**. Carefully he sewed the
mole's tiny claw back together.

"Thank you," said Wisgar. He
dived into his hole and popped back
up a moment later with a gift. "Please
take this **Golden Root** in exchange."

"Thank you,"
said Tibben.

He looked

at the map. He was nearly at Blue
Mountain, but he used Grandpa's
Super Speeding Potion to run
through the Green Silk Grasses
and save time. It seemed like
only seconds before he was at the
mountain's base.

Up, up, up he climbed, following
the steep path all the way to the
very top. An enormous crowd was
waiting – even King Krono was
there! The King stood regally among
the fairies and elves and goblins
and Cloud Giants and
knights

and druids and owls and centaurs
and dwarfs. Everyone had come to
see if the magical Potions Master
could stop the fearsome monster in
the valley below.

Tibben's tummy felt all jumpy
and jiggly. He was beginning to
wish he'd never left home.

"Um . . . hello," he said, and
everyone cheered.

"Ah, Potions Master." King
Krono shook Tibben's hand. "Thank
goodness you're here."

Tibben bowed low. "Um . . ."
he whispered to the
King. "I'm not really
the Potions Master.
I'm just Tibben the
Apprentice. See?
No Glints." He
waved his
cloak.

King Krono turned away from
the crowd and spoke quietly.

"Tibben," he said, "I know
Grandpa. He is a wise and clever
man. If he sent you, he must be sure
you can help." He put his hand on
Tibben's shoulder. "My kingdom
needs hope," he explained. "Every
time the monster growls, the land
shakes and the rock falls away. The
plants are disturbed, the animals
tremble and my people can't farm
the land. There is a strange mist in
the air and we are afraid."

Tibben shivered.

King Krono turned back to
the crowd. "Tibben is here!" he
announced. "He has come to

save us from the mighty beast!"

Everyone cheered again.

"The monster is down in Western Valley," the King continued. "No one has been brave enough to face it." He looked pointedly at his knights. They blushed and stared at the ground.

Just then there was an almighty howl from deep in the valley. The noise twisted up through the cracks and holes in the land. It crashed off the rocky cliff walls until it became a deep booming growl, filling the air. The land shifted sideways; bits of rock and soil crumbled and fell over the cliff edge, pulling plants with them. Everyone screamed.

Tibben's knees knocked together and he held his hands tightly behind his back to stop them from shaking.

"We know you will not fail us, Tibben," said King Krono.

The crowd cheered and clapped and raised Tibben up onto their shoulders. They carried him to the edge of the mountain and set him down.

Tibben turned to look over Western Cliff. No one

ever went right to the bottom,
he knew that. There was no
road, no path and no bridge to
get there. There was only one
way to reach the valley, and
that was to climb down the
crumbling cliff face.

Tibben gulped. All he wanted
to do was go home. But he
looked at the King, then at the
hopeful faces in the crowd, and
he realized he had no choice.
He had to help. He had to bring
back Harmony. He turned round
and gingerly stepped down
over the cliff edge. Bit by bit he
began to climb down. His toes
searched for footholds in the

powdery soil and
his hands gripped
tiny tree roots in
the earth.

Suddenly there
was another roar
from the valley
below. The land
trembled. The
ground gave way
and Tibben began to
slide! He scrambled
in a panic, but there
was nothing to hold
onto.

Down the cliff
he slid, down
towards the valley.

Chapter Six

Bump!

Bump!

Bump!

Tibben hit three bushes growing on the cliff face.

"Ow! Ow! Ow!"

He fell a little way further before landing on soft, muddy ground.

Tibben stood up and brushed himself off. He checked all over to see if he was hurt, stretching each limb one by one, and moving his head gently.

"Phew," he said. "I think I'm OK . . . but where am I?"

He looked around. He seemed

to be in some kind of hidden cave.
He peered out of the opening in
the cliff. He could see the valley far
below and the top of the mountain
a long way above. The bushes must
have broken his fall and thrown
him into this cave.

But then another thought occurred to him.

Was this where the creature was? Was the mighty beast here in the cave too?

Tibben shook with fear. "I can't do this!" he cried. "I'm not a brave knight. I'm not a soldier. I'm not the Potions Master! I'm just Tibben."

Then there was a noise.

"It's the monster!" he cried.

But when he listened again, the noise didn't sound like a ferocious roar, or an angry growl. It sounded like a whimper. Tibben lifted his head and listened again. There was another whimper. The beast sounded hurt.

"The monster is in pain, poor thing," Tibben realized, and he knew that he couldn't leave without trying to help it, however dreadful it might be.

He headed deeper into the cave, but no sooner had he turned the corner than he met a pile of rocks blocking the way ahead. He could hear the beast behind it. What could he do?

Then he remembered the visit
from Snark the Thunder Goblin a
few days earlier. Of course! Tibben
felt in his bag. There was only one
potion left – **ExplOding Powder**.
He lifted the jar high over his
head and threw it straight
at the wall, then
ran for cover.

There was an almighty noise as the rocks fell.

Tibben took a deep breath – it was time to confront the creature. He tried not to imagine its huge teeth. Or sharp claws. He tried not to think that its favourite dinner might be fresh pixie.

"Whatever this monster is," Tibben told himself, "it is in pain and I have to try to help it. Even if I can't make the right potion, at least I can see what's wrong.

There must be something I can do."
Tibben gulped. He climbed
over the crumbled wall to the
centre of the cave. And there,
sitting on a rock, was the beast.

Chapter Seven

Tibben started to laugh.

The beast wasn't a fearsome monster at all! She was a small, soft, fluffy thing, with huge eyes and a long tail. Trapped in the cave, she had been yelling for help, but her yells had echoed right across the cavern, down the tunnels and up through the holes and cracks in the land, until they sounded like almighty roars.

"Wooz," said the creature sadly.

Tibben could see that her paw was trapped under a heavy rock. He went to help, but the creature shrank back, scared.

"It's OK," said Tibben. "I'm Tibben; what's your name?"

"Wizz," said the creature.

"Wizz," said Tibben. "That's a nice name. Come with me, Wizz. I'll get you out." Gently he moved the rock and lifted her up into his arms. Wizz smiled shyly.

"You're going to be OK," said Tibben.

Back through the Secret Cave the two of them went, over the crumbled wall and through the

twists and turns of the tunnel.
Finally they came to the cave
entrance.

Tibben
looked down
the cliff side.
It was a long
way to the
valley below.
He looked
up. He would
never be able
to climb back
up the steep
slope holding
the injured
Wizz in his
arms.

The only way out was to fly.

Tibben shook his head as he remembered how every time he had tried to make **Flying Potion**, he had got it wrong.

"Help! Help! Help!" he called to the cliff above. But nobody came.

Tibben sat down on the cave floor with his head in his hands.

Just then there was a little squeak, and he felt a soft pat on his arm. Wizz was looking at him with her big blue eyes.

"You're right, Wizz," said Tibben. "We have to try."

He sat up straight. He opened *The Book of Potions* and turned to the recipe:

FLYING POTION

EFFECT: Allows flight of up to 30 metres for a period of 15 minutes.

INGREDIENTS: Light Puff, Cloud Lotus, Golden Root.

He took out his **Mage Nut** bowl and concentrated very hard.

"Not too much *Cloud Lotus*," he muttered to himself, remembering how he had accidentally made **Rain Potion**, "and I've got to stir it the right way," he said as visions of *Rooting Potion* filled his head.

Tibben looked at the potion nervously. "I hope it's right," he said to Wizz. "Otherwise we might be stuck here for a very long time."

He tipped his head back and drank. Nothing happened. He waited. Still nothing. Then, suddenly, his left leg lifted high in the air . . .

"Whoa," he cried, pushing it down. Up it rose again, nearly making him topple over. He sat down on his left leg to keep it still.

Nothing else was moving.

"Sorry," he sighed, shrugging his shoulders at Wizz. "It hasn't worked. I got it wrong again. I think I've made some kind of leg-floating potion." He looked very glum.

"Wooooz!" cried Wizz, bouncing up and down on her back legs. Her

tail was high in the air and, with her good paw, she pointed at *The Book of Potions*.

"I know; I know. I'm sorry," said Tibben.

But the creature pressed the book into his hands. "Wooooz woooooz," she said earnestly.

"Try again?" said Tibben, and Wizz nodded.

"OK," he sighed. "I'll try again."

Chapter Eight

Tibben gathered everything
together. This was his last Cloud
Lotus. He had to get the Flying
Potion right. He mixed carefully,
remembering everything Grandpa
had said.

Wizz danced up and down next
to him the whole time, her little tail
floating high in the air. He looked
at the fluffy white tail. As Wizz
bounced, the fluffiest bits of fur

flew off and floated around the cave.

"That's a very floaty tail," Tibben said. All he could think about when he looked at that tail was fluff and bounce and lightness. He remembered something Grandpa had said:

"Listen to the potion. Give it what it needs, even if the very thing it needs is not in the recipe."

Tibben looked at Wizz, and suddenly he understood what Grandpa meant. He could feel what the potion needed to make it work. It needed a little bit of fluff from Wizz's tail!

"Wizz," cried Tibben, "please could I have one of these bits

of fluff?" He pointed to a piece
floating in the air.

Wizz nodded fast and jumped up
to grab it. She pressed it to her heart
and handed it to Tibben, looking
into his eyes.

"Woo-ooz," she said in a serious
voice, and Tibben guessed she
was saying thank you to him for
rescuing her.

Tibben smiled at her, and carefully added the fluff to the mixture. Once again he lifted the bowl and drank. His tummy felt all warm as the liquid started to fizz. Bubbles rose up inside him, and he began to grow lighter and lighter.

"It's working!" he cried. Quickly he threw *The Book of Potions* into his bag. He slung the bag onto his back and pulled Wizz towards him as he felt himself lifting off the ground. "It's working!"

Tibben was flying. He leaned forward and nearly did a somersault. "Whoops!" he said, adjusting himself. He bent forward

more gently and they began to rise
up out of the cave.

"Woo-hoo!" laughed Tibben.

"Woo-zoo!" shouted Wizz.

Up and up they soared.

"Wow!" said Tibben. "I had no idea this potion would be so strong. We're flying really high – much more than thirty metres. I wonder why?" Then, suddenly, he realized: all the ingredients had been given

in gratitude! The potion was extra
powerful.

Tibben could see the Kingdom
of Arthwen spread out below him.
The east was green and lush, the
west rocky and mountainous. To
the north were the snowy plains

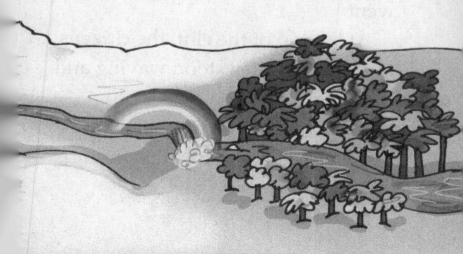

of the Frozen Tundra, where Frost
Trolls and Blizzard Bears stalked the
lands. The south was home to the
Parched Desert. Tibben could just
about see the sand dunes in the far
distance.

These were places Tibben had
only heard of in Grandpa's stories,
or read about in books. He couldn't
wait to travel across the lands just
like Grandpa had, helping all the
different creatures everywhere he
went.

At the top of the cliff, the citizens
of Western Valley stood waving and
cheering.

"Oooo!" the crowd gasped as
Tibben floated down to the ground.

"Wow!" said a little elf. "He really is a Potions Master!"

"Here's your monster!" said Tibben, smiling, and there was an enormous laugh when everyone saw the little creature cuddled up in his arms. This wasn't

the terrifying beast they were expecting at all! "Wooz wooz!" said Wizz happily as the children came up to stroke her soft fur.

"Well done, Tibben," said King Krono. "You were the only one brave enough to go into the cave."

Tibben blushed and everybody cheered.

There was a different feeling in the air – something fresh and clear. The land was stronger now; the soil was firm and hard and the plants shone with health. Tibben looked around the crowd. Everyone was smiling at him. Harmony had returned.

Tibben's heart filled with pride. He, little Tibben, Potions Apprentice, had brought back Harmony! Suddenly he couldn't wait to get home and tell Grandpa all about the cave, and Wizz . . . and how he had made his first **Flying Potion**! For the first time Tibben saw that Grandpa was right – he *could* do it. He could be the Potions Master one day.

Just then, Tibben glanced down at his cloak – there on the left side was a **Glint**! His first **Glint**! In all the excitement, he'd forgotten he would get one. The **Glint** was shaped like a hexagon and its shards reflected all the colours of the land – this was

Crystal, the first level of potions skill. Tibben's heart swelled – he'd reached Crystal! Finally! He turned his cloak this way and that, admiring the Glint shining out against the green fabric. Gently, he touched it with his finger. It felt sharp and hard, and as he ran his finger over its edge, it made a low humming sound.

"Wow!" he breathed.

"Woozoo!" said Wizz.

Tibben smiled and lifted Wizz up high. She was his lucky charm. "Thank you, Wizz," he said. "I'll never forget you."

Wizz let out a long sad "Woooooooz."

"Goodbye." Tibben sniffed. He gave her one last hug and walked away.

He walked a little. He walked a little more. Then he stopped. He turned back to see the little

creature looking at him sadly, waving her tail.

"Wait!" he called, running back to her as fast as he could. "Come home with me," he said, all in a rush. "Please come and live with me and Grandpa in our tree – you'll love it; you can bounce up and down the Potions Shop all day!"

"Woozoo!" said Wizz happily, and she flung her arms around Tibben's neck.

Chapter Nine

Tibben and Wizz had a long journey ahead of them, but the two new friends didn't mind. Tibben knew Grandpa wanted him to bring back as many ingredients as he could, so everywhere they went he picked and gathered. Wizz was very helpful – she was especially good at spotting all kinds of berries and roots.

In Moonlight Meadow they found Dew Drops and *Rainbow Blossom* for Glitter Dust. At the Green Silk

Grasses they picked *Lily of Loveliness* for Handsome Cream, and in the Cave of Darkness they gathered Grass Lichen for Camouflage Potion.

When
they finally
got home,
Grandpa was
waiting at the
door of the
tree to meet
them. He had
a huge grin
on his face.

"Well done,"
he said. "You did it!"

"How did you know?" asked
Tibben.

Grandpa patted the secret pocket
of his cloak. "The *Dial* is pointing
to H," he whispered.

Tibben beamed with pride. "And

look, Grandpa . . ." He showed him
the Glint.

"Crystal! That's wonderful!"
Grandpa smiled. "Only four more
to go!" He bent down. "And who's
this?"

"This is Wizz," said Tibben.
"She's coming to live with us . . ."

He faltered and looked at Grandpa. "Er . . . if that's OK?"

"Of course it is," said Grandpa. "Welcome to our home." He bent down to greet her. As he shook her little paw, a strange look came over his face.

"What is it, Grandpa?" asked Tibben.

"For a moment there I thought . . . Oh, never mind." Grandpa laughed and straightened up.

"Right," he said. "Now let's get back to it. I have so much more to teach you. Both of you." He looked at Wizz.

Tibben groaned. "Come on, Wizz," he said. "It sounds like

we have work to do."

"Wooz Wooz!" she chirruped, and bounced up the path.

Grandpa put his arm around Tibben and together they walked through the wooden door and into the tree trunk.

"You're going to be a great Potions Master," Grandpa said proudly.

"You know," said Tibben, "I really think I am."

Potions

Extracts from *The Book of Potions:*

Arm Stretch Cream
Effect: Lengthens arms
Ingredients:
- Stretch Thistle
- Fast Lotus

Camouflage Potion
Effect: Gives the drinker the ability to blend in to any background
Ingredients:
- Chameleon Claw
- Grass Lichen
- Silent Bark
- Glass Pearl

Cat Language Potion
Effect: Allows the drinker to speak to and understand cats
Ingredients:
- Sky Whisker
- Yowl Seed
- Thunder Rumble

Exploding Powder

Effect: Causes any substance to explode

Ingredients:

- Jumping Flint
- Fire Seeds
- Red-Hot Orchid

Fire Dance Potion

Effect: Makes the drinker dance till a spark appears

Ingredients:

- Red-Hot Orchid
- Jumping Flint
- Fire Seeds

Flying Potion

Effect: Allows flight of up to 30 metres, for a period of 15 minutes

Ingredients:

- Cloud Lotus
- Light Puff
- Golden Root

Glitter Dust

Effect: Rub an object with this dust to increase sparkle and shine

Ingredients:

- Diamond Powder
- Dew Drops
- Rainbow Blossom

Growth Potion

Effect: Increases size by 50 times
Ingredients:

- Giant's Eyelash
- Stretch Thistle

Handsome Cream

Effect: Makes the drinker 100 times more attractive
Ingredients:

- Glass Flower
- Chrysalis Powder
- Lily of Loveliness

High Reach Potion

Effect: Helps the drinker stretch to reach the tallest items
Ingredients:

- Stretch Thistle
- Giant's Eyelash
- Fast Lotus

Hover Potion

Effect: Causes drinker to hover for two hours
Ingredients:

- Golden Root
- Cloud Lotus
- Light Puff

Ice-Cream Potion

Effect: Paint any object with this potion to make it taste like ice-cream

Ingredients:
- Frozen Bloom
- Sugar Strand
- Berry Vine

Invisible Potion

Effect: Makes anything invisible for three hours

Ingredients:
- Chameleon Claw
- Glass Pearl
- Silent Bark

Magic Coal

Effect: Stimulates fire breath

Ingredients:
- Goblin Coal
- Red-Hot Orchid

Rain Potion

Effect: Causes rain to fall on an area of one square meter for three hours

Ingredients:
- Cloud Lotus
- Light Puff
- Dark Water

Rooting Potion
Effect: Sticks feet to the floor for two and a quarter hours
Ingredients:
- Golden Root
- Cloud Lotus
- Light Puff

Shrinking Potion
Effect: Makes the drinker shrink in size for 10 minutes
Ingredients:
- Vary Violet
- Mouse Water
- Low Root

Sticking Potion
Effect: Sticks anything to anything
Ingredients:
- Gumspider Web
- Red Clay
- Troll Slime

Super Speeding Potion
Effect: Increases speed by 1000 times for one hour
Ingredients:
- Fast Lotus
- Unicorn Whisker
- Quick Sand

Ten Legs Potion

Effect: Gives drinker 10 legs for a period of two hours, enabling them to run faster

Ingredients:
- Fast Lotus
- Quick Sand
- Stretch Thistle

Tidy Thread

Effect: Mends and repairs anything

Ingredients:
- Gumspider Web
- Troll Slime

Trail Powder

Effect: Improves tracking skills for 24 hours

Ingredients:
- Snout Grass
- Scent of the Valley
- Quick Sand

Ingredients

Extracts from
The Glossary of Magic Ingredients

Berry Vine
Grows in Moonlight Meadow; purple plant with small black berries. Used for **Cooking Potion** and **Ice-Cream Potion**

Chameleon Claw
Granted by Rainbow Chameleons on Blue Mountain after a favour is performed. Used for **Invisible Potion, Disappearing Potion** and **Camouflage Potion**

Chrysalis Powder
Ground from abandoned butterfly houses in Moonlight Meadow. Used in **Beauty Potion** and **Handsome Cream**

Cloud Lotus
Floats on Lake Sapphire; white fluffy plant. Key ingredient in **Flying** and **Floating Potions** as well as **Dreaming Potions, Hover Potion, Rooting Potion, Waterskate Powder** and **Rain Potion**

Dark Water
Found in caves. Used for **Rain Potion** and **Cooling Potion**

Dew Drops
Collect from Moonlight Meadow. Used for **Glitter Dust** and **Shine Potion**

Diamond Powder
Made from grinding diamonds from the Diamond Mines. Used for **Glitter Dust, Sharpening Ointment** and **Shine Potion**

Fast Lotus

Found on edge of the Green Silk Grasses; thin, sharp plant always covered in Racing Snails. Used for all **Speed Potions, Ten Legs Potion, High Reach Potion** and **Arm Stretch Cream**

Fire Seeds

Pick these from the Burning Flower in the Parched Desert. Used for **Fire Dance Potion, Super Strength Potion** and **Exploding Powder**

Frozen Bloom

Grows in the snow on the Frozen Tundra; silver flower made of snowflakes. Used in **Ice-Cream Potion** and **Numbing Potion**

Giant's Eyelash

Exchange with Cloud Giants on the Peak of Peril for **Grace Potion**. Used for **Growth Potions** and **High Reach Potion**

Glass Flower

Rare ingredient found in palaces. Used in **Beauty Potion, Handsome Cream** and **Transformation Gel**

Glass Pearl

Fish for these in Lake Sapphire. Found in transparent oysters. Key ingredient in **Invisible Potion, Disappearing Potion** and **Camouflage Potion**

Goblin Coal

Given by Thunder Goblins under Blue Mountain in exchange for **Exploding Powder**. Key ingredient in making **Magic Coal**

Golden Root

Grows underground in Moonlight Meadow; look for golden flower and dig under left side. Used for **Flying Potion, Floating Potion, Hover Potion** and **Rooting Potion**. Store underground

Grass Lichen

Grows under rocks in the Cave of Darkness; green moss-like plant. Used in **Camouflage Potion**

Gumspider Web

Found in Steadysong Forest. Take one strand at a time only. Used for **Sticking Potion, Climbing Potion** and **Tidy Thread**

Jumping Flint

Found in the Diamond Mines under Blue Mountain; silver-coloured stone. Used in **Fire Dance Potion, Mop Dance Gel** and **Exploding Powder**. Beware – this stone will leap about once cut!

Light Puff

Taken from the breath of a dragon. Used in all **Flying Potions, Hover Potions, Rooting Potion** and **Sweet Tune Potion**

Lily of Loveliness

Grows in the Green Silk Grasses; bright white plant. Used for **Beauty Potion** and **Handsome Cream**

Low Root

Found in Moonlight Meadow. Used for **Shrinking Potion**

Mouse Water

Collect from Mouse Pond. Used for **Shrinking Potion**

Quick Sand

Covers the ground at Mouse Pond; take care when collecting! Used in all **Speed Potions** and **Ten Legs Potion**

Rainbow Blossom

Grows in Moonlight Meadow; plant of seven colours. Used for **Glitter Dust** and **Shine Potion** and for **Beauty Potions**

Red Clay

Found at the bottom of Lake Sapphire and Bubble River. Used for **Sticking Potion**

Red-Hot Orchid

Grows in Steadysong Forest; ruby-coloured petals. Do not touch the leaves. Used in **Fire Dance Potion, Exploding Powder** and for making **Magic Coal**

Scent of the Valley

Found in Steadysong Forest. Used in **Trail Powder**

Silent Bark

Peeled in Steadysong Forest from the hollow Silent Bark Tree. Key ingredient in **Invisible Potion, Disappearing Potion** and **Camouflage Potion**

Sky Whisker

Exchange with Sky Cats of Blue Mountain for Essence of Milk. Used for **Pouncing Potion** and **Language Potions**

Snout Grass

Found in the Green Silk Grasses. Used for **Trail Powder**

Stretch Thistle

Grows in the Green Silk Grasses. Tall green spiky plant. Used for **Growth Potions, High Reach Potion, Arm Stretch Cream** and **Ten Legs Potion**

Sugar Strand
Exchange with Sugar Bees in the Green Silk Grasses for Super Speeding Potion. Used for **Kindness Potion** and **Dessert Potions**

Thunder Rumble
Extract from the base of Blue Mountain during a thunderstorm. Used for **Language Potions** and **Weather Potions**

Troll Slime
Grows under bridges in Troll Hills. Used for **Sticking Potion, Climbing Potion** and **Tidy Thread**

Unicorn Whisker
Exchange with Twilight Unicorns on Moonlight Meadow for Diamond Powder. Used in all **Speed Potions, Hair Potions** and **Regeneration Potions**

Vary Violet
Found in Frozen Tundra.
Used for **Change Potions**

Yowl Seed
Furry Yowl Plant grows in the Green Silk Grasses. Distinctive orange and black stripy fur.
Used for **Language Potions** and **Monster Fur Cream**

About Tibben

Arthwen pixies are born in Pixie Pouch Trees in Steadysong Forest.

Pixies start their life very small; at first they are little joeys, each wrapped in a soft, furry leaf of the Pixie Pouch Tree. They nibble on the leaf for food, and as soon as they are big enough, they nibble their way out and land on the forest floor below.

After that, most young pixies head for Moonlight Meadow or the Green Silk Grasses, choosing the green lands around Steadysong Forest.

But for some reason, when Tibben fell from the Pixie Pouch Tree, he felt a strong urge to wander further into Steadysong Forest.

Grandpa was outside the Potions Shop that day, watering the plants with Growth Potion.

When Tibben saw Grandpa, he was curious and he stopped to ask him lots of questions. And as Grandpa talked to him he got a funny fizzy feeling inside; he knew that Tibben would be the next Potions Master. He asked if Tibben would like to become his apprentice and Tibben said yes.

Tibben's adventure continues
– read on for a sneak peek of

The
Magic
Potions
Shop

The
River
Horse

Chapter One

Deep in Steadysong Forest was an enormous tree. It was the biggest tree in the Kingdom of Arthwen and its vast trunk was hollowed out to house a very special shop: the Potions Shop. This shop was where goblins came to get **ExplOding Powder** to help them in the Diamond Mines. It was where dragons bought Magic Coal for their belly fire, and where imps came for *Invisible Potion* so they could play all kinds of mischievous tricks.

At the top of the tree were three little bedrooms. In the first one a pixie called Tibben was just waking.

He stretched and yawned. The sun was already creeping across the wooden floor and it was time to get up. Customers would start arriving soon, travelling from all over Arthwen to the Potions Shop.

Tibben yawned again. The shop had been so busy lately! Every day creatures came, needing creams and ointments and oils and potions. Grandpa was the Potions Master. He was the one who made all the different remedies and cures. He travelled the kingdom, from the Frozen Tundra

to the Parched Desert, visiting creatures and helping them.

Tibben was the Potions Apprentice. It was his job to help Grandpa, to study and to learn. Then, one day, when Grandpa retired, Tibben would take the Master's Challenge to become a Potions Master himself. Tibben was studying hard, practising new potions every day. He had already earned one **Glint** – the magical sign of potions skill. As he pulled on his cloak, Tibben could see the **Glint** shining out brightly against the plain green fabric. It was only one, but it was a start. Tibben couldn't wait until his cloak sparkled with hundreds of **Glints** of all shapes and sizes, just like Grandpa's. Four more **Glints** to go, Tibben told himself as he opened his door, then I can take the Master's Challenge!

He had promised Grandpa that this morning he would work on *Jumping Potion*, after yesterday's disaster, when he'd added too much **Bouncy Moss**. The potion had only worked on his left shoulder, and he'd spent the whole day twitching like he had fleas.

He tiptoed down the corridor, trying not to wake Grandpa, who had been up till late last night picking **Red-Hot Orchid** in Steadysong Forest. Tibben could hear soft snores coming from behind his door.

In the next room along Tibben could hear Wizz leaping about. He smiled – Wizz could never keep

still! The branches of the tree shook
as she whizzed around, jumping
from bed to sofa to wardrobe to
window. Wizz had only recently
come to live with them, and Tibben
was glad she had settled in so well.
She seemed to love helping in the
Potions Shop, and every day she
was getting better and better at
talking.

He knocked. "Wizz? I'm going down to practise."

"Wizz come! Wizz come!" she cried. She flung open her door. Her huge blue eyes stared up at Tibben and her tail quivered in excitement. "Catch Wizz!" she shouted. She rushed past him and down the spiral stairs in a blur of white fluff.

Tibben laughed and followed her all the way to the shop.

"I'm making *Jumping Potion* again," said Tibben as he lifted his special **Mage Nut** bowl onto the counter. Wizz winked and made her left shoulder twitch. "Very funny," said Tibben. "Hopefully I can get it right this time."

Wizz dashed around the shop
fetching all the ingredients for
Tibben. She was so quick! She could
leap from shelf to shelf in the blink
of an eye and, even though there

were thousands of jars and bottles and tubs and pots holding all kinds of plants and seeds and flowers, Wizz could find anything Tibben needed.

"Wow! Thanks, Wizz," said Tibben as she set everything out on the counter. There was the **Bouncy Moss**, a balloon-shaped plant that grew in Moonlight Meadow, and

the *Leaping Lily*, which had to
be fished out of Bubble River at
dawn while the flower was still
sleepy enough to be caught. Wizz
had even brought a flagon of **Fire
Fuel Hops** down from the very top
shelf, holding it in her tail, without
spilling a single drop.

Tibben concentrated on mixing
the ingredients together. He was

careful not to put in too much **Bouncy Moss** this time, and he chopped up the *Leaping Lily* quickly before it leaped away.

"Hmm," said Tibben, "I wonder how much **Fire Fuel Hops** to add. I might just pop upstairs and ask Grandpa." But Wizz shook her head. "I know, I know . . ."

Tibben wasn't supposed to check everything with Grandpa. He was supposed to try to make the potion himself. He added a few drops of **Fire Fuel Hops**. Then a few more.

Tibben and Wizz peered into the bowl.

"What do you think?" asked Tibben.

"Weeeeez," said Wizz.

"I don't know either," said Tibben. "I'm almost scared to try it."

"Wizz try! Wizz try!"

"Are you sure?"

"Wooz!" Wizz nodded and took a sip.

For a moment nothing happened, but then . . .

WOOZOO...

"Woozoo!" cried Wizz as she shot straight up into the air.

"Oops," said Tibben. "Definitely too much **Five Fuel Hops**."

"Weeeeeeeee!" Wizz called as she flew round and round the Potions Shop like a balloon running out of air. Tibben could hear the *clink, clink, clink* as she bounced off one jar then another.

She was getting
faster and faster
until . . .

Splash!

She landed in a
large tub of Troll
Slime.

Her little head popped out of the
tub, dripping with the bright green
goo. Tibben started to laugh. Wizz
started to laugh.

"Oh Wizz," gasped Tibben.
"What a mess!" He handed Wizz a
towel to wipe herself down with.
Then, together, they worked to
clean up the shop before customers
started to arrive.

Turn the page for lots of fun

Magic Potions Shop

activities!

Word Scramble

The names of some of the people and places in the
Kingdom of Arthwen have got jumbled up! Can you
restore Harmony by unscrambling them again?

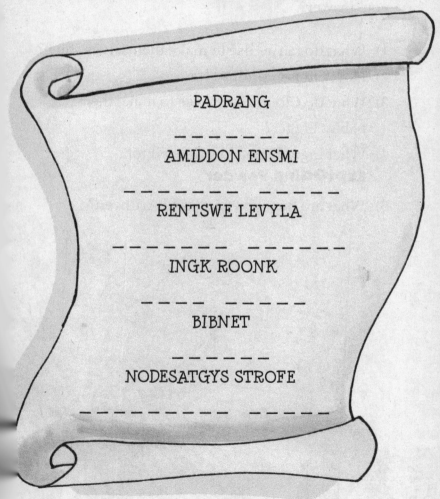

PADRANG

_ _ _ _ _ _ _

AMIDDON ENSMI

_ _ _ _ _ _ _ _   _ _ _ _ _

RENTSWE LEVYLA

_ _ _ _ _ _ _   _ _ _ _ _ _

INGK ROONK

_ _ _ _   _ _ _ _ _

BIBNET

_ _ _ _ _ _

NODESATGYS STROFE

_ _ _ _ _ _ _ _ _   _ _ _ _ _

Turn to the back of the book for the solution to this puzzle!

Tibben's Quiz

Test your knowledge – how many questions can you answer?

1) What do fairies use to make themselves shine?
2) How old is Grandpa?
3) What do Cloud Giants use to make their babies bigger?
4) What ingredients do you need for **ExplOding Powder**?
5) What are the two energies of Arthwen?

6) Who writes to Grandpa asking for his help?
7) What is the name of the creature Tibben helps?
8) What extra ingredient does Tibben add to make **Flying Potion**?

Turn to the back of the book for the solution to this puzzle!

Follow the Trail

Stocks of *Rooting Potion* are running low in the Magic Potions Shop – can you follow the trail to help Tibben find Wisgar, the Specs Mole, who has some **Golden Root** so that he can make some more?

Turn to the back of the book for the solution to this puzzle!